Milo Moves Away

written and illustrated by Sami Paul

Book Bunny
Publishing

For my bunny, Milo

Published by Book Bunny Publishing

ISBN: 978-1-7357838-2-6

Hello, my name is Milo
and I've got a lot to say.
I'll tell you about my
old home and why we
had to move away.

My mom and dad and me lived inside a cozy tree with a big round table and a lot of food to eat.

My friends and I went to a little school under a shady tree where the soil could stay cool.

When I wasn't in school, I liked to roam among the trees and look up at the sky to watch the butterflies and bees.

But one early morning I woke up with a start; I heard a loud noise so I ran out in a dart. And when I looked up, afraid of what I'd see, I found a two-legged creature cutting down our tree!

Afraid of the creature, I quickly hopped away, but when I stopped I saw a sight that worsened my bad day!

Our school had been destroyed along with the rest of our town, and all we could do was sit and watch and frown.

We stayed a while longer, but in about a week, concrete began to fill our meadows and our creek.

We asked the two-legged creatures to leave but they refused, so we packed up all our things, said goodbye, and moved.

All the animals from our town had to travel a long way, but after a while we found a new place to stay.

We made a new school and new burrows and new dens, and we went to the new school with new pencils and new pens.

And every night I fell asleep feeling safe now that we lived in a wild, untouched place.

But one early morning I woke up with a start; I heard a loud noise so I ran out in a dart.

And when I looked up, afraid of what I'd see, I found a two-legged creature about to cut down our tree!

But this time was different, this time was new, instead of one two-legged creature this time there were two.

But the second one didn't have an axe in his hand; his job was to protect the trees and forest land.

He got the first one to leave in less than a minute, because he protects the forest and everything in it.

So I hopped back inside, happy as can be, knowing we were safe in our new cozy tree.

The End

CPSIA information can be obtained
at www.ICGtesting.com
Printed in the USA
LVRC021547071220
673536LV00020B/235

9 781735 783826